For ks
Christmas 2005

The Bird in Santa's Beard

How a Christmas Legend Was Forever Changed

By

Jeffery L. Schatzer

with Mark Bush and Don Rutt

Illustrations by Ty Smith

Big Belly Books
Midland, Michigan

www.BigBellyBooks.com

Big Belly Books
P.O. Box 1254
Midland, MI 48641-1254

www.BigBellyBooks.com

ORDERING INFORMATION:
Individual sales are available at select booksellers and retail outlets. For information on locations or to order via the internet, contact Big Belly Books at the address above or at www.BigBellyBooks.com. Special discounts may be available on quantity purchases by corporations, associations, charities and others.

Printed in the United States of America
A Product of the Great State of Michigan

Library of Congress Cataloging-in-Publication Data

Schatzer, Jeffery L., 1949-
The Bird in Santa's Beard: How a Christmas Legend Was Forever Changed/ Jeffery L. Schatzer – 1st ed.
1. Christmas Story – Fiction.   2. Photography – Fiction

Library of Congress Control Number: 2004091312

ISBN: 0-9749554-0-X 51995

First Edition

2004

To the wonder of belief

Believe Forever!
Santa

t happened the year that a cold, cold

winter had settled in the North. The birds

had long since flown to their warm nesting areas . . .

all the birds, that is, except one.

s Santa was on his way to look in on the reindeer, a squeaky little voice called to him. "S-S-S-Santa, I am f-f-f-f-freezing," a tiny bird chattered.

"Come, warm yourself in my beard," Santa said kindly.

Frup-frup-frup, the bird's wings flapped as it fluttered into the fluffy beard.

rudging through the deep snow, Santa sheltered the bird from the bitter wind.

Upon returning home Santa made hot chocolate and oatmeal with cinnamon. When the bird poked its head out to look around, Santa asked, "Would you like some?"

The bird chirped in delight.

hey talked as they shared their warm meal.

The bird peeped about how much fun it is to fly high in the

sky. Santa agreed and spoke of how much fun it is to ride in his sleigh.

Suddenly, the bird became quiet and looked very, very sad. "What

shall I do? All the other birds have flown south, and I am all alone."

"Please stay with me," Santa said. And

that's exactly what happened.

hroughout the winter Santa and the bird became the best of friends. The bird even built a nest in Santa's beard. At bedtime Santa was careful to sleep with his beard and the bird outside of the covers. The bird didn't mind that Santa snored.

One December morning, Santa woke to loud chirping sounds.

"Santa!" The bird flitted and fluttered with excitement.

"Wake up! Look and see! There are eggs in my nest."

ater that morning Santa whistled as he polished his big black boots. "Santa, you must be quiet and still," shushed the bird.

Suddenly Santa realized he had a big problem. "What shall I do? Every year before Christmas I visit with the children. Sometimes the children are noisy. Sometimes they wiggle around. I do not want to disturb your eggs, but I do not want to disappoint the children either."

I t was a big problem indeed.

Santa thought and thought. The bird thought

and thought. They both thought and thought until

their thinkers couldn't think any more. Suddenly the

bird peeped and flapped her wings. "You have many

grown-up friends. Perhaps they can dress to

look like you and visit with the children.

They can be your helpers!"

"hat a wonderful idea!" said Santa. "Why,

they can tell me who has been naughty and

who has been nice. They can also let me know what

the children would like for Christmas."

Together they talked to Santa's friends.

The grown-ups enjoyed dressing like Santa and visiting the children. The bird even helped by reading letters. Still, what was to be done about Christmas Eve? Santa just couldn't deliver toys with eggs in his beard.

n that magical night the bird chirped the answer softly into Santa's ear. "Though my eggs have not yet hatched, they are now strong enough to be moved. You must take my nest out of your beard. Please place us somewhere safe and warm. Then you can deliver toys to the children tonight."

anta smiled a big smile, and gently he combed

his fingers through his beard and lifted the nest.

Carefully he carried it over to the Christmas tree.

Softly he placed it on a sturdy branch.

ust before Santa flew off in his sleigh that night, the bird warbled a beautiful Christmas song. Her music was one of the most wonderful Christmas gifts Santa had ever received.

he eggs hatched the next morning. It was

Christmas Day. Santa enjoyed the company of

his bird guests that entire winter. In the spring the

birds said goodbye and joined their friends. From time

to time, the birds return for special visits with Santa.

Family reunion —
Last Christmas
Birds (left to right):
Maurice, Mama Clara,
Julius, Baby Ramona

o this very day, children often wonder why so many different grown-ups dress like Santa and help him at Christmastime. Now you know why.

It's because of the bird in Santa's beard.

Deepest Appreciation

To Mark and Corrine, Don and Pat and to my loving wife, Deborah, thank you for believing and giving so freely of your support and energy. Special thanks to Ty Smith for adding so much to this project. To Sam, Josh, Allyson, Jesse, my "special editor", to the instructor and students of OAT 155 and the students and teachers of Good Shepherd Lutheran School in Midland, thank you for your thoughts and insight. Special thanks go out to our bird friends: Maurice, Mama Clara, Julius and Baby Ramona. (We hope you have a safe and enjoyable migration.) To Ashleigh, Nathan, Raychel, Natalie, Madison and Danny, you continue to inspire through your love. Finally, to Mary Ida and Nate, Tom and Holly and all those who give life to the Spirit of Christmas, special thanks for your work at spreading joy in a troubled world.